Jump!

by Sheila Sifton
illustrated by Kristin Goeters

Harcourt

Orlando   Boston   Dallas   Chicago   San Diego

Visit *The Learning Site!*

www.harcourtschool.com

Lamara grumbled to herself. "In a month I'll be nine. When am I going to get this right?"

She gripped the rope handles with both hands and bent her elbows. The rope went over her head and past her face. It went down in front of her and she jumped. She spun the rope again, but this time it hit her in the back of her head.

"OK. Here I go again. One, two, three, and jump and . . ." Lamara stopped. The rope had hit the front of her ankle. "One jump. I can never get to the second jump!"

Lamara slumped down on the step.

"Hi," said Hope, sitting down.

"What's the matter?" asked Virginia.

"Nothing," answered Lamara.

"Will you take an end?" asked Hope, holding out the end of a rope to Lamara.

"Sure she will," said Virginia. "I'll take an end, too. You jump first, Hope. Let's start with Snakey, Snakey."

Virginia and Lamara bent down and wiggled the rope back and forth. Hope jumped from side to side. She started jumping near the end of the rope by Lamara and jumped back and forth all the way down to Hope's end without stepping on the rope.

Next Lamara and Virginia shook the rope while
Hope jumped. Then it was Lamara's turn to jump.
The snake never touched her. She was grinning when
she took an end from Virginia.

"Low Water, High Water!" called Virginia.

Lamara looked puzzled, so Hope said, "Just put
the rope on the ground like this." Virginia jumped
over it. "Now hold it up a little higher." Each time
before Virginia jumped, the two girls raised the rope
a few inches. After five good jumps, Virginia's foot
touched the rope. Hope took her turn. Then Lamara
took a turn.

"Now let's do Bluebells!" said Virginia.

Hope and Lamara swung the rope back and forth.

Bluebells, cockle shells,
Eevy, ivy, over,
My dog's name is Rover,
One, two, three, sugar, coffee, tea.

Then Hope took her turn jumping as Lamara and Virginia chanted with her.

To Lamara's amazement, when it was her turn she jumped and didn't miss until she got all the way to *sugar, coffee, tea.*

"I have to go home pretty soon," said Virginia. "I can stay for one more set. Let's do ONE and." She stood in the middle, next to the rope on the ground.

This time Hope commenced to turn the rope over Virginia's head, but Lamara didn't get her end of the rope high enough.

"Wait a minute," Hope said to Virginia. "We have to practice turning the rope." Virginia stepped out away from the rope. Once Hope and Lamara were turning smoothly, Hope nodded to Virginia and she went back into the middle.

The turners turned, and the three girls chanted in rhythm to Virginia's jumps. She jumped a big jump on the number and a little jump on the "and."

ONE and	*SIX and*
TWO and	*SEVEN and*
THREE and	*EIGHT and*
FOUR and	*NINE and*
FIVE and	*TEN and STOP!*

"So long," said Virginia. "It's time for supper. See you tomorrow. Your turn first then, Hope. Bye, Lamara."

When Lamara was by herself, she said, "ONE and TWO and THREE and," as she went up the stairs and into the house, "FOUR and FIVE and SIX and."

"What are you counting, honey?" called her mother.

"Nothing," answered Lamara. "SEVEN and EIGHT and NINE and . . ."

Her mother smiled. She remembered that kind of counting.

"It's my turn to jump first today. Let's do ONE and," said Hope. She jumped, but missed on NINE. "You're supposed to miss on how old you are," she told Lamara. "Virginia is ten, so she's not supposed to miss at all. Your turn Lamara."

They turned and Lamara jumped. "... SIX and SEVEN and EIGHT and ... I didn't miss. I stopped on my age," she said.

"Right," said Hope. "My turn. I choose Tap Your Head."

Hope jumped and did some motions with her hands, as she and Virginia chanted.

Tap your head, tap your nose
Tap your chin, tap your toes.
Tap your knees. You're almost done,
Clap your hands, and out you run.

When Lamara jumped, she didn't do the hand motions. She was concentrating too hard on jumping. When she missed, nobody said anything.

"Let's jump Teddy Bear," said Hope.

This one had motions too, kind of hard ones. At the end, each jumper ran out. Lamara watched closely. When it was her turn, she jumped but didn't turn around.

Teddy bear, teddy bear, turn around.
Teddy bear, teddy bear, touch the ground.
Teddy bear, teddy bear, tie your shoe.
Teddy bear, teddy bear,
You better skiddoo.

Hope chose the next chant. It had motions too.

Old Ben Franklin went to France
To teach the ladies how to dance.
Bow to the duchess, curtsey to the queen,
Salute to the captain of the submarine.
Wave to the duchess, wave to the queen,
Wave to the captain of the submarine.

The next day Lamara's mother said, "How about the three of you going over to the school playground with Olivia and me? Hope and Virginia can call home and see if it's all right to come along with us."

At the playground were two other girls they knew.

"Hey, want to jump rope with us?" called Virginia.

"Sure," Lucy answered "I'll take an end. Let's jump Mississippi Push."

Lamara took the other end and began turning. Virginia and Hope both ran in and jumped together, facing the same way.

"What are they doing?" thought Lamara, but she kept turning as they chanted.

Down the Mississippi
Where the boats go PUSH

On the word PUSH, Helen tapped Virginia on the back and Virginia jumped out. Hope jumped in. The girls kept jumping in and out until someone missed.

Then Helen taught them a new chant. She told them to jump in on their birthday month.

Apple, peaches, pears and plums
Tell me when your birthday comes.
January, February, March, April, May, June,
July, August, September, October,
November, December

The girls continued in this way all spring and summer. Whenever they could, they jumped rope. After practicing with Hope and Virginia all spring and summer, Lamara was a very good jumper.

One fall day at the playground, Lamara noticed a younger girl watching the three of them jumping rope. Lamara asked the younger girl to take an end, and she did.

One Teaches Another

How do children learn to jump rope? Most often they learn from other children. They learn in playgrounds and on sidewalks. They watch older children, and then they join in. If they are fortunate, older children might invite them to jump in. Sometimes, they are summoned to turn the rope for older friends.

The chants have been passed from generation to generation. Children listen to the chants. The chants have rhythm, and sometimes they rhyme to make them easy to remember.

Perhaps you have learned to jump rope. Perhaps you would like to learn. If you are interested, find a flat surface to jump on. You must have enough space for the rope to turn. You must not give up. You must try persistently. It's important to be faithful and practice often.

It is not easy, but once you can jump you'll have so much fun. There are jump rope clubs and jump rope competitions for teams of jumpers. If you live near a playground that has lights, you and your friends will never have to stop jumping! So,

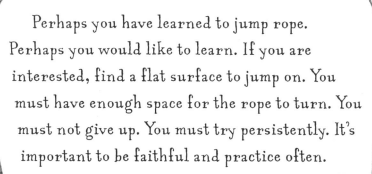

HAPPY JUMPING!